PREFACE

All proceeds from the sales of 'All Roads Lead to Malton' will be donated to the Teenage Cancer Trust, UK.

The T.C.T. helped my daughter, Laura, ten years ago, when she was a patient at St James' Hospital in Leeds, where she, thankfully, survived a lymphoma.

Every day seven young people aged 13-24 hear the words: "You have cancer. They will each need specialised nursing care and support to get them through it. The Teenage Cancer Trust is the only U.K. charity dedicated to meeting this need.

"No young person should ever have to face cancer on their own."

John Botterill   February, 2023.

INTRODUCTION

'All Roads Lead to Malton'   **John Botterill**

One of my earliest memories is when I once abruptly sat bolt upright in bed, and tried to conceive of any places beyond my own village, Rillington, and the local market town, Malton. I also considered how would I get to these mythical places and I also struggled with the issue of why I would even want to go, given that all my imaginable needs were adequately satisfied in my local area. I was not, clearly, a curious or a well-read child!

As it turned out, there **were** quite a few interesting places that were not Rillington, or Malton, and there were roads (and railways) connecting us, more or less directly, with them. Who knew? I certainly didn't!

The roads which take us out of a town, though, can also lead us back there; or at least, they can if we want them to. As I have become 'more mature', I have reflected on my life and those early experiences seem to occupy a far more prominent place. I can see, now, how my grandchildren are currently being shaped by their formative years and this has encouraged me to wander down Memory Lane. Malton has become like Rome, and all my roads have led me back there. Good job it's not a bad old place!

If I was ever tempted to be at all pompous about this collection (not in my nature, of course!) I would assert that what I have created is impressionistic, rather than realistic. I have applied a dash of colour here and there, with broad, but not intricate, dashes of the pen. I believe that I should be judged as much by the intention as by the achievement!

My aim has been to understand my own life, my truth, by reflecting upon it. My aim was that readers would find some echoes of their own experiences in my poetry, whether they hail from Yorkshire or not.

 Any road up, 'I did my best.   I sincerely hope that you enjoy taking this journey with me.

I have, by the way, timed the release of 'All Roads Lead to Malton,' to coincide with our neighbouring city, Leeds, becoming the U.K.'s City of Culture for 2023. Leeds is very much part of this story and was, indeed, one of the most important places which, I discovered, existed beyond Malton. I went to University in Leeds, I support the football team (for my sins!) and Laura, my daughter, was treated for her lymphoma in Leeds' hospitals. Leeds is a fine city, well-deserving the great accolade which has been bestowed upon it.

#Culture Around Every Corner

John Botterill.   February, 2023.

Contents:

PART ONE: "Let's get this party started!"

Part Two: "Could you keep the noise down, please?"

Afterword.

Books by this author.

PART ONE   (AN UPHILL STRUGGLE)

"Let's get this party started!"

Waiting

Let me take you back to the start,
of the West Mids College drama production.
As luck would have it,
I landed the plum part:
Estragon, a dim-witted stooge
for the cerebral Vladimir,
in Beckett's 'Waiting for Godot.'
It was a role, my friends, which suited me fine.
Typecasting was alive and well,
In 1979.

I enjoyed the knockabout humour,
the badinage, the quickfire exchange
of insults, intensifying
until we wounded each other,
mercilessly. A marriage, of sorts.
Vladimir was not, of course,
as clever as he thought.

Life reflects Art. Art reflects Life.
At the time I entirely missed the point,
when life was still so young and sweet,
as a newcomer to life's pain and strife,

I was a willing victim of the chancers
whom I chanced to meet, with their myriad
of promises they made and never kept.
I was indestructable, though, and undeterred,
why should my gratification be deferred?

How long have I been waiting
For my time to begin?
Life is a game of poker
and it has not dealt me in.

"What, then, shall I say of this day?"

That I am still here waiting, waiting still,
Under this old, decrepit tree.

Perhaps then tomorrow, maybe,
Mister Godot will come, for me.

2. Blood Man

Four doors down on Malton Road
on the way towards Scarborough,
lived my nana and grandpa.
I toddled around there often,
as they were usually quite kind to me,
and let me watch their new T V.

Early on, I was two or three,
I was shocked by a scene in their kitchen!
A figure sat slumped in my dad's overalls,
as large as life, on the top of the fridge,
weirdly, he was wearing red lipstick,
on his mouth and on his nose,
A woolly hat perched, on top of his head,
and, suddenly, a thought arose.
"Blood Man! Blood Man!"
Is what I said.

His odyssey did not end well.
We took him into the garden
and burned him on a pile of wood,
with shouting, dancing and merry cheers,
as rockets emblazoned the dark night sky.

It bothered me for many years.
In all my restless dreams,
Blood Man came to visit me.
I sobbed at the sight of his agony.

His legs were stuffed,
with paper and clothes,
whilst blood poured out,
from the end of his nose.

I wondered what poor old Blood Man had done.
What ghastly crimes deserved this torture?
And why did we gather, with such delight,
every year on Bonfire Night?

3. The Winter of '63

I am tunnelling down, into my memory,
heaving mountains of compacted snow,
clearing away the misconceptions,
applying an ice pick as I go…

The dawning of an Ice Age: the Winter of '63.
An eerie silence, in those days long past,
when we were cut adrift by an Arctic blast,
no cars were moving in, or out,
we clapped our hands, to keep them warm,
and wore our coats inside the house.

I fashioned a path through the frozen snow,
a fearless youngster, with nerves of steel,
whose face was frozen, whose fingers could not feel,
I dug on, though snow was above my head,
wielding a spade, last used on a beach!
The blizzards blew! I was undeterred!
The huskies had fled, I was beyond their reach!
No search parties came, I was on my own,
in the coldest Winter I had ever known!
An intrepid explorer who defied the cold!
Forging a Northwest Passage, through to Nana's,
which was four doors down, on Malton Road.

When the snow falls, now, around our way,
and my grandson shouts, "It's snowing! Hooray,"
warmly muffled in his hat and coat,
I quietly smile, as I'm tempted to say,
"Call this SNOW? These powdery flakes are NOTHING!
You should have been digging, alongside me,
clearing Rillington's North West Passage.
back in 1963!"

4. Malton Museum

'Visit Malton Museum.'
I read a dog-eared leaflet, from off the floor,
'Malton is nothing but a museum,'
I grumble, along Yorkersgate,
'And that's a statement of the truth!'
Past 'The George' and The Palace Cinema,
those relics of my misspent youth.

I turn into a Market Place,
which only the sixties could own.
Preserved in aspic, set in stone.
This is some weird time warp,
Where 'Doctor Who' meets 'Heartbeat'!
I kneel to retie my Jesus Boots
and glance up to greet an icon,
"Ah Mister Herriot, I presume!"

A town lost, in its own antiquity!
Where all is kept as it has always been,
a triumph for the Conservation Team!

I find myself, suddenly, in Greengate-
my early Nemesis, my infant Fate-
outside the Friends' Meeting House,
the scene of my first day at school,
and my first proper telling off!

I quake at the snarl on Miss Smith's face!
All my yesterdays began in this place,
where I left the group of tiny extras,
to join the supporting cast.
I was mortified by the admonishment!
It would not be my last!

And Malton remains unaltered,
a museum to my past.

5. All at Sea

My school career did not start well.
No one explained how school should go,
they must have thought me rather 'slow.'
Saint Katy's Roman Catholic Primary School
did not spare the rod nor suffer the fool.
I tried hard to listen. I just wasn't able.
I struggled with even my three times table.
I couldn't stay quiet when teacher was talking.
I bumped into trees when I was walking
to school, heaving my bag.
To be honest, I found that school was a bit of a drag.

Cut far adrift from the safety of home,
at the mercy of rip tides and gurgling foam,
I was soon treading water and gasping for air,
The school offered discipline; what I needed was care.

St Katy's had an ethos transformation!
Each classroom table was shown as a ship, at sea.
A ship en route to the 'Rewards Treasure Island.'
This change in St Katy's was a revelation,
As the island held treats and goodies galore.
As a six year old child, who could want more?
Good work guaranteed your table's progression,
Bad behaviour retarded your table's propulsion.
But, this scheme left daydreamers all at sea,
On the flotsam and jetsam of their reverie,
Daydreamers who looked a lot like me...

Needless-to-say, our ship didn't fare well,
we began going backwards at the sound of the bell.
"Turning around, John. One space back."
"John, you're not working. One space back."
"Talking too much, John. One space back."

My table was livid, they were on the attack.
"John! Be quiet! Has your brain gone slack?

I was all at sea. All at sea.
And, like the ancient mariner,
every one of them blamed me!
Our ship was in the doldrums- we couldn't move on-
all because of the Jonah, they all knew as John!

So, the treats of Treasure Island eluded us.

The anger of classmates' comments, still echo in my mind.
I listen to memories of their baleful chorus,
"John! John! You won't let us move on!"
The endless chidings which were correct, if not kind...

no wonder I preferred the home-bound bus.

6. A Lesson for Life

Two small trees, at both ends
of our tidy, sun blessed, lawn,
defined our very own Elland Road.
The goal mouths, ragged and worn.
One-a-side was a murderous match,
helter-skelter, to and fro.
To a passer-by, it must have looked mad,
but I was only seven years old,
and it was me versus my dad!

At nineteen all, the scores were level.
Next goal's the winner, we both knew.
I was confident, full of swagger,
I'd faced this jeopardy many times before.
I'd beat my father, I'd surely score!
Winning bliss!
I'd so got this!
I ran the ball towards the trees,
took aim- but then-he'd tackled me!

I ran back, quickly, to no avail!
My dad had scored, he didn't fail.

Twenty- nineteen! The game was done.
My dad had disappeared inside.
I stood on the lawn, I wailed and cried!
I was the victim of a heinous crime!
"Come out and play, dad, extra time!"

"No, sorry, son. The game is over.
Just this once, I'm afraid you've lost."

All my pleadings were in vain,
it was a lesson in life's growing pains.

Twenty- nineteen was a painful score
but, looking back, I know it hurt him more.

I stood there, shouting, "I want a replay!"
"John. I've said, that's enough for today!"
I just had to take it on the chin.
Life is a game, like football,
where you cannot always win.

7. Confessional

The genesis of my narrative invention,
began in the throes of Catholic confession.
What counted as a sin?
Where should I begin?
"I have disobeyed my mother
seven times, father,
I have used bad words
three times, father."
The numbers were arbitrary.
the sins, venal.
I had to have something to confess.

"Two 'Hail Marys' and an 'Our Father.'"
The priest passed sentence
and, at the tender age of seven,
I emerged, purged.
Should I have suffered bad luck
and been hit by a truck,
I would still have gone to heaven!

I confess that I did lie to the priest!
I hadn't disobeyed my father or mother,
Or repeated any unchristian rhymes!
I really had no use for sin, at the time.

Children were forced to search within
for any possible secret sin.
This was not about forgiveness -
It was more concerned with control.

Peering into every child's soul,
making us fixate on our guilt,
until we are frail and old...

Father, it is fifty-five years since my last confession.
My unrepented sins have banked up,
like a coastal shelf, against a flooding tide.
They are too many and too various to innumerate,
my blackened soul has been abandoned to fate.

'Doubt and confusion' describe what I feel.
I have prayed to God in darker times,
balancing my atheism with a Christian zeal.

So, please add hypocrisy to the list of my crimes.

8. The Birthday Party

To cement my bonds of friendship,
with Peter and Geoffrey and Glenn,
I invited them to 'my' house
for a birthday party, way back when.
Sun shone down from that August sky,
the scene was set, and hopes were high!

A wild pack of youthful hyenas
pawed, restlessly, at our front door,
with new-washed faces and hopeful smiles,
we couldn't have asked for more!

They dashed through to the kitchen,
to help themselves to cake,
and careered on into the garden
to see what a mess they could make!
Town dogs let loose in the country
and scenting all manner of crime,
my pals, Peter, Geoffrey, and Glenn,
were lovely lads, most of the time!

Geoffrey Bobbles Bonbon
climbed high into a tree,
removing all the apples

to throw them down at me!
They wrecked our ancient furniture,
in a brash game of musical chairs.
A tennis ball, thrown in a game of tag,
caught a greenhouse window, unawares!

My dad came out to survey the carnage
and, with a sad shake of his head,
he picked up some pieces of wreckage,

"What? Call this a party?" he said!

I would call all my friends 'misguided,'
rather than outright 'bad,'
suffice it to say that this party,
was the first, and the last one, I ever had!

9. A Fishy Story

Dad went to Bridlington, fishing.
It was one of the things he did.
He would come back home with tales of the tides,
the rise and the fall of the sea,
the rainy squalls and the cries of the birds,
describing the way fish would hide
underneath the shadow of the boats
He talked about bait, and weights and floats,
the way men were seasick, at the edge of the deck

As many fine tales as an old seadog could wish.
Yet, despite all these powers, we seldom saw fish!
An empty car-boot once caused mum to say,
"It's not just the big ones which got away!"
But, like the wedding feast at Canaan,
There was a miracle in store.
On the day my father's boot was full,
and, in a large box on the back seat,
was a plastic bag containing even more!

The grin that he wore,
as dad got out of the car,
Went right across his head.
It was the story of loaves and fishes,
except he didn't produce any bread!

Yet, to my dismay, the fish were all dead!
A profusion of grim death lay on the kitchen table!
All with bulging, staring glass eyes,

their mouths wide open in aghast surprise
capturing the moment of their sudden, sad demise.

We gave them away to our neighbours.

Though, I'm not sure they found them a treat.
"With all those heads and fins, bones and skin,
are they safe enough to eat?"

10. Rillington Playing Fields

Old style leather footballs, with laces,
were murder to maneuver, when wet.
They soaked in all the water,
and, if you tried to head it,
you nearly broke your neck!
And yet, and yet…
'Tot' Temple and 'Woodbine Wilf' Oxendale,
the stars of our Rillington football team,
would flick it back and forth to each other,
as though it was as light as a feather,
and fire it, unerringly, into the back of the net.

In Rillington there was no thought of holding back.
Each match was a battle, there to be fought.
In a tackle, leave your foot in!
Get your retaliation in first!
Football is not just about taking part!
A win, is a win, **is a win**!
These were my rites of passage,
where I learned the Rillington code.

I stood, once, behind the netting,
on a crisp, cold Winter's Saturday,
at a Scarborough and District League game.
Near the end, Tot Temple broke free.
He blasted the ball left-footed,
and directed it straight at me!
I was protected by the netting
as Tot's shot thundered in.

I was amazed by Tot's great poise and power.
Entranced by his skill and amazed at his grace.
He'd aimed the ball at exactly the right place!
But mostly I was just dumbfounded.

How could he generate any propulsion at all, upon such a **heavy ball?**

11. First Night Nerves

My first night match was in '67.
Dad took me along to Elland Road.
I thought I'd died and gone to heaven,
when I saw how the floodlights glowed.
I stood high on a wooden box he had made,
bringing me level with the height of the crowd.
I caught a glimpse of the manicured grass,
and the myriad white scarves, fringed with blue and gold.
Oh, the mayhem, the uproar, and the jubilation
when Jimmy Greenhoff scored his goal!
One -nil against Liverpool - just the job!
I felt cocooned amidst the baying, tuneful mob!
And, for a while, Leeds United were in control,
When Giles popped up with the second goal!
Delirium, bedlam, hysteria!
It thrilled me to my very soul.

Then – it shook me to my foundations,
the referee pointed to the penalty spot!
He's given handball against Bremner!
The anger, the rage, the rabid indignation!
"The ref's not right in the head! He's not!"

Penalty converted. It was now 2-1
Two minutes to go. The pressure was mounting
and in my head, it's the seconds I'm counting!

The gut-wrenching, buttock-clenching tension,
a cry of despair! The ball's kicked high in the air!
There's a pain in the pit of my stomach.
My head is now beginning to ache.
Oh, the goalie has come out to claim it.

A magnificent goalie called Sprake!
We're down to only a minute to go.
"Come on, ref, blow your whistle! Blow!"

It's over! It's okay! We've done it! We've won!
I breathed my first gasps of air for a while,
"Wow! Thanks, dad! Now wasn't that fun?"

Being him, he just stood there and smiled.

12. A Funny Old Game

Is the love for a football team,
A blessing or a curse?
A nightmare or a dream?
Or a drain upon your purse?
More enduring than marriage,
More pervasive than sex,
Your team demands constant attention,
For very little reciprocation.
The endless permutations,
Which scores ensure our survival?
Or, more unlikely, success?

The love for a football team
Is scarred with heartache, pain
And careless, cruel deceptions,
Alongside brief, intermittent, joy.
You hold your hope close, like a guilty secret,
And it is the hope which kills you, finally.

But Love is never quite so unrequited,
As when your love is for Leeds United!

13. Different Times

Those were different times,
when father put his pay packet
onto the kitchen table
every Thursday night,
for mother to count,
whilst retaining a share,
for fags and beer.
When money was put in tins,
on the mantelpiece,
for the never-ending bills.

Smoke curled out from our fireplace,
to mingle with smoke from his fags.
The smoke was blowing everywhere.
We breathed in, deeply, the blue-tinged air.

Different times.

He would stub out fags
between his calloused fingers
and his bulbous thumb,
and aim the nubs, haphazardly, at the fire.

Some struck their glowing target,
but most lay ash-strewn on the hearth,
awaiting the dustpan and brush.

I was sent, as a budding cold-war spy,
On 'secret missions' to Westgate Garage.
"Twenty Players and a box of matches,"
he whispered conspiratorially.

"Here's a ten-bob note, but I want the change!"

Once, later, when we were round at nana's,
the change from a one-pound note
emerged, like a magic trick, from my pocket.
Instinctively my father turned around,
amazed at the ten-bob note he espied.
"Here! That'll be mine," he said.
As I was permanently penniless,
this just couldn't be denied
and, sadly, I was rich no more.
Player's Navy Cut were his brand.
Unfiltered. Full strength. Lethal.

A throwback to his Second World War,
marooned in Malta on the 'Aurora,'
They gave them out, then, buckshee (free)
To ward off the terror.

Different times.

Maybe I helped to kill him,
with those legal drugs I bought.
Nobody knew the harm back then,
The ravages cigarettes wrought.

Or maybe they did,
and the evidence was hidden,
So that at least the businesses survived.

Different times.

14. A History Lesson

As a child, I found a stinking gas mask,
consisting of decaying rubber and plastic.
Uncomfortable though it was, I tried it on,
constricting my breathing. As under a deep sea,
I saw my sister, laughing...
I didn't keep it on for very long!
I flung it back into the drawer,
with all the farthings and the ha'pennies,
and a ration book; redundant relics
from the Second World War,
which no one had thought to throw away.

Our past accumulates. It banks up,
like the soft rock strata in a coastal cliff.
Lower down in the drawer, had I but looked,
were some pieces of scrimshaw
and battered, old workhouse records,
a cavalry sword and a blunderbuss,
some bows and arrows and a hard flint tool...
tenacious tendrils of the roots which made us.

It's not just a subject which we learn in school!
Whatever we do. Whatever we say,
history clearly filters through,
into every strand of our DNA.

15. How to not learn French

The problem of how to speak and write in French
was deemed somewhat esoteric
at Norton Secondary Modern School,
akin to learning how to solve quadratic equations,
or the tedious business of saying please,
and thank you.

Physics? The periodic table? Really?
It was surprising how many subjects
could be enthusiastically jettisoned,
if you really put your mind to it.
The names of English kings and queens?
How to play music, or how to dance?
But, learning French, Mon Dieu,
what was the point,
if we were never going to visit France?

This was the burden of our anguished cry
as we bounded up the stairway to room thirteen.
Unlucky for some, as might be thought.
Well, unlucky for our teacher, Mr Green,
and for me!

Learning French was inutile!
Whoever heard of feminine verbs?
Or wanted to visit a boulangerie?
French was all double Dutch to me!
Yet Mr Green made me take it at C.S.E.

Then, promptly left, replaced by Mr Cross,
an aptly-named man who frequently asked me,
"Whose side are you on, John?"

"Je ne comprends pas," was my sly reply.

So, failure was etched onto my Life's C.V.
Sans joie, sans succes, sans Espoir,
Pour tout l'eternite.

16. Scarborough Cricket Festival

"Scorecards! Cards sixpence each!
Get your scorecards here!"
The old man in the white coat was always there,
his booming voice echoing around the ground.

Balmy, sunlit weekdays at the festival.
Bright azure blue, and cloudless, skies.
Not even the merest breath of a breeze.
Seagulls squawking, eyeing up our sandwiches,
as we lay out our picnic on a rickety old bench.
Happy, happy days on North Marine Drive.
The twack of leather upon willow.
Dizzying white flannels against the green.
The cricket pavilion, of splendour,
which I scoured for glimpses of my heroes!

And I saw Graeme Pollock rattle off a ton,
the fastest century of the season by a mile!
This wizard whirled his bat round, like a wand,
caressing the ball to all parts of the ground,
suddenly, dispatching it over the sightscreen!
Where I caught it!

Metaphorically. Fifty years too late.
And where I now serve it up,
on Memory's plate...
"Scorecards! Scorecards! Cards sixpence each!"
Happy day! Oh, happy, happy day!
It was T. N. Pearce's Eleven versus Yorkshire.
We didn't need a scorecard, anyway.

17. Not Long Ago

On the double seats in the Palace Cinema,
with a tense new girlfriend, out for a show.
Trying to make sense of 'Enter the Dragon,'
our sweaty hands became entwined.
Did she want me to kiss her?
I just didn't know.
I carefully eased her face towards mine,
and I shared her cherry-flavoured chewing gum,
for an hour or two!
Not long ago...

Time passed on and we didn't go back,
like 'Enter the Dragon,' we faded to black...

The "wonderful smell of Brut!"
or a splash of Hai Karate,
but I was "careful how I used it,"
as it drove young ladies wild!

I watched Brucie on 'The Generation Game,'
whilst Anthea did her twirl,
before we went to the Milton Rooms Dance,
wearing stacked heels, like Slade.
It was yet another search for a girl
and we always thought we had it made!
"Get her number and then give her a call!"
We were Mercutio and Benvolio,
off to the Malton Capulet Ball!
Not long ago...

It seems like only yesterday-

Or perhaps a little bit more-
Chatting, about girls, with compadres,
working out what all the courting was for,
"Life is the name of the game!"
And it was all out there, for us to explore.
But, when I closed my eyes for an instant…

there was no one left on the dance floor…

18. An Academic Reflection

Steve and I were friends, at Leeds University.
We shared a taste in beer and music,
and a healthy disinterest in Philosophy.
We casually lounged about in tutorials,
or meandered off to the lecture hall,
or sought some solace at the Union bar.
Two dilettantes spending, unwisely,
Our much-vaunted, ill-gotten student grant.
Remember them?
We were "wasting hardworking taxpayer's money,"
so my dad said.
It was great!

We had the leisure to consider questions
of purely academic interest, in smoke-filled rooms.
Steve would lean back thinking, deeply,
Or pretend to, whilst drawing on an Embassy,
before releasing thought-filled plumes.
"A radiator is seventy per cent water.
I am seventy per cent water.
Am I a radiator?"
Absurd! Preposterous!
It all appeared such a delicious waste of time!

Looking back, though, on reflection,
university was an oasis, a brief hiatus,
before those terrible twins,
those relentless juggernauts called
Work and Responsibility rumbled on through.

19. Rillington Motor Cycle Club

It was the era of Mods versus Rockers.
Scooters, Ben Sherman, and Parka coats,
motorbikes, Levi's, and slicked-back hair.
Pumped up teens, who thought they were hard,
fighting in lumps on the promenade,
during sunny sixties bank holidays.

Rillington, my village, was solidly greaser,
not a single scooter was ever seen
a Motorcycle Club of our very own,
where lads picked tarmac out of their jeans.

Whilst, notionally, a Bike Club member,
a few obstructions blocked my way,
"There's nothing there between you and the road,"
said dad, with the air of a man who knew,
a chap with a definitive point of view.

"He fell off his Triumph every weekend,"
was what Uncle Harry had to say.
Motorbike ownership, then, was a forlorn task.
Was a leather jacket, though, too much to ask?

My friends at school all called themselves Mods.
Affiliation was more complex than I thought.
New idols challenged my local gods.
I was caught in the crossfire of no-man's land,
when mods and rockers' battles were fought.

And so goes the story of my life.
My allegiances would come and go,
I played both ends towards the middle,

when I was faced with trouble or strife,
a man who likes to hedge his bets, undecided,
about people or places to loath or like.
One of Life's Motorbike Club members,
who never bought a leather jacket
or, more crucially, a motorbike!

It wouldn't take a detective to see
a lack of authenticity
or a want of commitment to a cause,
when my friends say, "Come on! Let's go!"
I will press 'Pause...'

❖ ❖ ❖

20. Let's Cycle in Yorkshire

A song, written to celebrate the Tour de Yorkshire in 2019.

Let's cycle in Yorkshire
Green trees and vales.
Go cycle In Yorkshire,
steep hills and dales.

Get those long legs pumping,
It's what a strong heart needs.
Get your big heart thumping,
through Bradford and Leeds!

Let's cycle in Yorkshire!
It's a great place to be!
Go cycle in Yorkshire!
from the hills to the sea!

The folks are all charming,
and we're modest as well!
Cos our humour's disarming,
as I'm sure you can tell!

And the weather's delightful!
Not a dark cloud in view!
If you happen to see one,
we'll paint it all blue!

When you're riding around here,
as you'll be happy to do,
not much to beware of,
except a pot hole or two!

Let's cycle in Yorkshire!
Flat caps and beer!
Go cycle in Yorkshire!
The pies are all here!
The race will be fair, like,
banned drugs will be few!
But, if you want to be lead bike,
take the M62!

Let's cycle in Yorkshire!
How broad we all talk!
Go cycle in Yorkshire!
Through Selby and York.

Explore Nature's Bounty!
In God's own county
Tha'll stop feelin' nowty
In twenty nineteen.
Where the lush grass is green,
and the grey skies turn blue!
Go cycle in Yorkshire!
We're waiting for you
Go cycle in Yorkshire!
We're waiting for you....

◆ ◆ ◆

PART TWO (DOWNHILL ALL THE WAY)

"Excuse me, but would you mind turning the noise down, just a fraction. Thanks ever so much!"

21. The A64 Blues

I got the driving back to Malton,
on the tedious A64 blues!
I can't listen to the radio,
I don't want to hear the news!
All the dire warnings,
about all the endless queues!
I got the driving back to Malton,
on the tedious A64 blues!

Stuck behind some tractors,
and a mobile port-a-loo,
I've missed yet another meeting,
This is a right fine how-do-you-do!
I got the driving back to Malton
on the tedious A64 blues!

Don't blame me for my road rage,
because there is just no end in sight.
I'm in a caravan convention
and they block me, just for spite.
I'm sitting here biting fingernails,
watching the green grass as it grows,
counting cars as they fade into the distance,
with their drivers all picking their nose!

Come to Yorkshire for our scenery!
Come on, take in all the views!
I got the driving back to Malton
on the enervating, nauseating, tedious
exhausting, A64 blues!

22. Can I be Frank?

My dad was a journeyman joiner,
who worked, with a saw in his hand.
He wore his blue overalls, proudly,
a dedicated, skilful artisan.

He never raised his voice to us,
let alone his powerful fist.
His silent disappointment was enough
to point out the duties we'd missed.

My father led by example.
Deeds, not words, were his way.
"Faults you see in others,
Correct in yourself!"
Was what he used to say.

In our village, Frank ran the youth club,
a leader who gave them his prime,
he knew how to help all the youngsters along,
a prophet ahead of his time.
My father left an indelible mark-
I've thought of this, many times since-
with his love of poetry, drama and art,
he was a modern-day renaissance prince!

Frank's memory stands towering over me,
his influence becomes greater, not less.
My aim to become like the man he was,
is a measure of my dad's success.

23. The Journeyman Joiner

Dad's overalls were a tatty shade of denim blue,
held together, over his shoulders, by a silver clasp.
He kept a rectangular pencil behind one ear
and a Player's cigarette behind the other.
Frank would eat his sandwich at a workshop bench.
For a journeyman joiner, it was catch as catch can,
and he was proud to be a working man.

Frank's tools were scattered across the shop
and they seldom saw the bottom of his bag.
Yet dad fashioned order out of this chaos,
and he didn't see this mayhem as a snag.
"Why would I waste my time tidying up?
Here! Go boil a kettle and fill me this cup!"

Frank liked to focus on the task in hand.
His woodworking projects were seldom planned.
He mentally visualised the end results.
A staircase, a wardrobe, a dining chair,
all built to order, or lovingly repaired.

A ciggy would burn at the end of his bench
or smoulder, benignly, behind his ear,
as he, laughingly, scoffed at the notion of harm,
"A nice little fire would keep me warm!"

Dad was a veteran from the Second World War,
who knew only too well, what true peril was like,
and he didn't need a foreman to tell him his job.
Smoke went on rising, molten ash fell on the floor,

the tinder dry shavings all seemed ready to burn.

His jobs were waiting, he had money to earn,
and Frank didn't believe he had lessons to learn.

24. The Chisel

I stood and watched my dad, entranced,
as he chiselled a hole into a table's leg.
The chesil was a wand in this strong man's hand,
As he strove to make that table stand.

His hammer met the chisel's head, precisely,
Time after time, and time after time again,
carving and slicing into the wood's bright grain.
Until he brusquely brushed the shavings away,
like a conjurer performing his trademark trick,
as a perfect mortise was revealed below,
before a hand-sawn tenon was glued,
and slotted in, hard tight.

            I looked on, amazed,
dumbfounded, at what my dad could do,
with two bits of wood and a smidgen of glue.

25. Twenty Minutes to the Bell

Tired old teachers never die,
they just come back again on supply!

I know I am in trouble,
when I keep glancing at my watch.
A bead of sweat rolls down
my furrowed brow.
A hand shoots up.
"Yes?" irritated teacher voice,
"What is it now?"
"Can I go to the toilet?
I am desperate. I need a pee!"
Laughter. A belch and then a fart.
Raucous laughter
Some of them can belch and fart at will.
A paper aeroplane glides across the room.
What am I doing here? Teaching, still?
And when did bodily functions become funny?
Wife of Bath's Tale. Geoffrey Chaucer. 1400.
I answer my own question.
I didn't expect that they'd know.

I send my lado toilet bound.
Against school regulations!
He's been released onto the corridor!
I'm hoping he isn't found!

I'm glancing at my watch again.
"We need to finish this essay today," I say,
injecting a sense of pace and rigour.

I notice a couple of louts, mouthing obscenities
and grinning inanely.
'Do not advertise poor behaviour,'
my internal manual advises.
I say nothing, as I look at my watch again.

Bringgggggg! The fire alarm ringgggs!
My saviour! Bringggggg!
I escort my cage of pent-up lions towards the door,
carefully directing them away
from the non-existent fire,
gleefully escaping this dreadful, teaching mire.
I sign the forms and then, happy day,
I can finally retire.

26.   A Walk, to Remember

Mum's Care Home, being next to the cemetery,
Allows for some mawkish pursuits,
like my health-giving walks among the dead!
This encouragement to physical exercise,
it suddenly occured to me,
is also an exercise in egocentricity.

In my morbid ramble between these stones,
I search for those I may have known.
Based on the dates of their demise,
or names remembered from my youth.
My feelings, as I peruse these graves
are complicated, ambivalent and confused,
but what is poetry, if it tells not the truth?

'We glimpsed you briefly through the trees
But you blew away in the morning breeze'

This epitaph brings tears to my eyes,
enough to make me sympathise,
momentarily.
But, in the end, it is all about me.

Life is lived, our lives our viewed,
through the prisms of our own content.
Does each one's death diminish me?
Does ego's dominion ever relent?

For whom am I weeping if not for me?
A sense of relief. I outlived my friend.
A sense of dread,

I will join him there, in the end.

One day, someone will look down and say,
"I was at school with Johnny B!
He hasn't lived as long as me!"

27. History is Bunk

The past is always being reinvented,
edited, revised, amended, purged.
We would recoil, in absolute horror,
if something closer to the truth emerged.

Our tethered lives, our scatty brains,
the grubby compromises made from Day One,
the fighting out of bombastic battles,
until only our battered shells remain,
fleeing home, through the driving rain.

Most days are best swept under the carpet,
consigned to the garbage bin,
we are glad that they are gone.

My past- the event I choose to remember-
is that day in Malton, when then the sun once shone...

28. Reunion

A Tuesday night in The Union Pub.
Willy, Gareth, Ian, George and me,
like members of an aging rock group,
settling down, convivially,
to discuss our imminent comeback tour.
A manly hug, as we reached the door,
and we felt a glow of friendship,
like bathing in the summer sun.

We drank our Yorkshire bitter
and relived all the fun!
Refought all the battles
to make sure that we had won!

We dusted off our memories
for a helter-skelter fairground ride
of flashing lights and swirling beer,
to have lived all this, gives a sense of pride!
Rolling back the long-gone years,
suddenly we were back there again,
when we were boys not stocky, grey men!
These treats are just stored, lads,
they're archived, not gone.
A few beers and reminiscence!

Nostalgia! It's a tonic available to everyone!

29. What Nana would have said

Nana was small, but forthright.
You were never in doubt about
what this pocket battleship thought!
She liked to keep her purse strings tight
and the 'Cost of Living,' was the battle she fought...

Two pounds fifty for a sausage roll.
What would Nana have had to say?
"Don't try and take me for a fool!
Come again, I wasn't born yesterday!
When is this madness going to stop?"

A fiver for a pint of beer?
"Well, I'll go to the foot of our stair!
They should come and try to live round here,
If they think that the cost of living is fair!"

A five-pound note for a slab of butter?
In my mind's eye I can see my Nana mutter,
"Pull the other one, lad, it's got bells on!
You can shove that Lurpak where the sun don't shine!"
Twelve quid, now, for a bottle of wine!
"Do you think I've just fallen off a flitting?
That's far too dear, from where I'm sitting!"
95p to post a letter!
"I'd think you were daft, John,
if I didn't know you better!"

Nana died in 2002.
But I can hear her, now, inside my head
and her words of wisdom still ring true.

The Consumer's Champion is not yet dead!

30. Shadows

I sit here, in the graveyard of my dreams,
weeping stupid, futile tears,
for friends whom I have never known,
the chances I let pass me by
and for all the places I have never lived.

I did not live in Wentworth Street
and view Saint Leonard's lonely church,
haloed by the setting sun,
or wait in glorious trepidation,
for my lustful, new lover to come,
whilst sipping on her coke and rum.
This is the life I did not live.

Instead, I filled out puerile forms
and answered the insistent phone,
to forge a career of my very own,
climbing, daily, the greasy pole,
marching up work's windy hills,
cooling my passion and youthful ardour,
as managers gripped me by the throat!

So, I cry salt tears for those days, remote,
for memories I can never now have
and for the deathless poetry,
I never wrote.
As existence elapses and the sands of time
flow rapidly down towards the gap,
a fathomless sorrow grabs my soul.
Each grain of the sand is a friend unmade,
an open goal that I cravenly missed.
I should have done so much more with my life,
than this.

JOHN BOTTERILL

31. An Elergy, written in New Malton Cemetery

In New Malton, there is dignity in death,
when you have coughed and hacked your final breath.
A single bed to sleep in, on your own,
horizontal, blameless, alone, in peace,
in regular, neat rows of fine-cut stone,
with plastic flowers at your head.
A dignity, denied to the living,
is generously bestowed on the dead.

Even the falling leaves obey the clear symmetry,
in this immaculate, fine cemetery.
There is seemliness and stately order,
a spare summation of a life well spent,
at odds with the chaotic lives, these graves oft frame.
There are no dark struggles, here, to make ends meet.
No endless arguments, with frantic heat.
Death expresses kindness, and gives you your name.

32. The Gift

I've read through all my poetry,
it's full of angst and doubt.
If you're feeling pain, John, show it!
Go on, sunshine, let it out!

And yet, I've been so lucky,
born at a fortunate time,
After the war and before climate crisis,
not much in the way of violent crime!

Brought up in a backwater idyll,
cherished and nurtured by family and town,
given food, security, friendship and love,
Not much there to make a man frown!

This very lack of deprivation
has robbed me of perspective.
Set free to fight perceived injustice
and let loose my invective!

Yet, I know how much I was valued,
supported, taught, and understood.
Brought up to respect the rule of law
in a calm and peaceful neighbourhood.

It's the gift that goes on giving
-my father's words, here, still hold sway-
"All right, John, you can have your say,
but you must stand your round,
and pay your way!"

33. Hide and Seek

Grandad's garden is huge.
It has lots of places to hide.
Behind the tree, within the shed,
Behind that ginormous bush!
Eyes closed; I have counted to ten,
A trick I have learned from TV.
"Grandad! Where ARE you?"
A faintly distant reply comes
From somewhere in the garden,
"You have to find me, William."
A pause. A rustle in the bushes.
"It's the whole point of the game!"

My garden is far too small,
For a decent game of hide and seek.
There's no point kneeling behind the wall,
And the foliage is too sparse and bare.
Crouching beside this evergreen bush
Hurts my knees and my bulging girth,
Clearly protrudes from the undergrowth!
A dead giveaway! The attraction
Of hide and seek palls after a while,
But returns, on seeing William's
Beaming smile.
"Found you, grandad!"

"Everybody's out on the run tonight,"
I sing, like Springsteen, to myself.
"But there's no place left to hide!"
Happily, though, I go back to our game.
"It is your turn to hide, William,
Grandad will count to ten!"

34. Early Learning

"One more jelly baby, grandad,
then it's over, final... finish."
William swept his arms, flatly,
across his infant chest,
in a gesture of finality,
that I could believe in
and cherish.

I watched, as the sugar-coated treat,
disappeared before my very eyes,
as he seemed to swallow, rather than eat.

Another day, another school run.
William, bedraggled with bag and coat.
His mind had turned to food and fun.
A smile bedecked his cherubic face.
He patted my pockets where jelly babies hide,
discovering, immediately, a certain trace,
the outline of my delicious tribe.

"Just four jelly babies then over, finish,
I am four years old, so I need four more."
His logic is cast-iron and unarguable,
as four more of my jelly babies vanish.

So, what has William learned?
How to harvest the world's resources.
The delicate principles of negotiation,
within the framework of a modest ambition.
The benefits of incremental drift.
How smiling avoids a relationship rift,
about being concise about one's demands,
and getting the goods into your hands,
before trying to raise the ante again.

He holds his fingers and thumbs up into the air.
"But four was then, grandad, now I need ten.
Then it's over with, finish..."

◆ ◆ ◆

35. Shapes

"Shapes are everywhere, grandad. EVERYWHERE!
There's a triangle, here's a square!"
William pointed through the moving car's window.
He had said all this with an air of surprise,
but this challenged me to open my eyes,
to see this world, with the mind of a child.
Yes, shapes ARE everywhere, it cannot be denied.
I was impressed by his delineation
(He only turned four yesterday!}
and by his fascination, at God's creation!

"My face is a circle," William said, into the mirror,
"An oval," I corrected, as only a teacher would.

Our senses dim, as we grow old.
We lose our wonder for all we behold.
It's all around, the magic is STILL THERE.
It takes a child, though, to show us where.

36. Monday Afternoon

I met our glorious new grandchild,
on a sunny, Monday afternoon.
We were formally introduced,
though, initially, she was halfway
through a fascinating snooze.
I was instantaneously besotted!

Juliet nestled on my shoulder,
listening, intently, to nursery rhymes,
discovering meanings in the stories I told,
glancing, askance, from the side of her eye.
This genius of learning, only three weeks old,
extended her lungs as she started to cry.

Her beating heart was connected to mine,
on a Superfast Broadband to the soul!
A pristine addition to our growing clan!
I felt Power in her fingertips,
I found access to the Spring of Truth,
An electric charge surged through this old man,
As though she had whispered, "Grandad, SHAZZAM!"

37. Happy Birthday to...Me

It's got to the stage
of my mother,'s old age,
where I buy all my own cards
for her to address, and sign,
when she can summon up the energy,
when she can spare the time.

So, I bought myself the birthday card
I wanted to receive,
the one I thought I truly deserve,
although some may wonder
at my nerve...
A line of superheroes bedecked the top,
Hulk, Captain America, Ironman, the lot.
"You're not just a Superhero,
You're a Super Son, as well..."
Self-praise, though, is no recommendation.

I offered it for her to sign, with trepidation.
'Flipping Heck,' she wrote in her spidery hand!
You would have to know her, to understand.
I go back home to connect to my roots!
"Be a good boy!" and she signed the card, "From Mum."

And so now, I know, I am still her 'little boy,'
who has grown too far big for his boots!

38. Our Christmas Tree

The Christmas tree decorations,
as much as my mother and I,
speak tellingly of the ravages of time.
The tree, which we bought at Woollies,
was once a dark and lustrous green
and is now a grubby chocolate lime!
The tinsel, unlike me, is decidedly thin.
The baubles are cracked and hazed.
The pottery Santa has a cheery grin,
but he's lost his adornment of snow.
The fairy is still holding her withered wand,
but her gossamer wings fell off and flew west,
 in a childhood Christmas, long ago.

But these are mere embellishments
and it's a miracle that they've survived!
They symbolise longevity,
the fact we're still alive.
This ancient tree is standing,
embellished with our memories,
from the painted cardboard elves below,
to the fairy lights above,
this tree remains, enduring,
just like a mother's love.

❖ ❖ ❖

39. My Mother, waving goodbye

I could see her on the first-floor landing,
as I drove off, from the car park below.
Her hand was raised, waving gladly,
 as she peered, blindly, towards me,
with eyes which had long ceased to see.
A mother's smile was on her face,
Epitomising all her love and grace.

I stopped the car, to dab my eyes,
she would never see the tears I cried,
when I spotted my mother, waving goodbye

40. Still Waiting

Life is but a waking dream,
surrounded by a fitful sleep.
We stagger around, to get Life started,
but it's over with, before it has begun.

I have been ambushed by the setting sun.

What, then, shall I say of this day?

That I lived, I loved, I met with friends,
but Godot did not come,
even though I waited,
waited until the very end.

Mister Godot sees me from above,
the deity of parental love...

"Ah! My son is sleeping yet.
I shall wake him, in a little while.
He will tell me of all the troubles he's got!
Some of his dreams, he may have remembered,
but most of them, he will have forgot!"

AFTERWORD

All proceeds from sales of this book will be donated to the Teenage Cancer Trust.

Every day seven young people aged 13-24 hear the words: "You have cancer. They will each need specialised   nursing care and support to get them through it. The Teenage Cancer Trust is the only U.K. charity dedicated to meeting this need.

"No young person should ever have to face cancer on their own."

BOOKS BY THIS AUTHOR

Released On Licence (Poetic Licence)

Written under the pseudonym, J.G.Barwell.
A collection of poetry, some comic, some serious on the subjects of
life, death, family life in a wide variety of styles and approaches.
Something for everyone!

Printed in Great Britain
by Amazon

18389189R00047